Tiger has a Tantrum

Written by Sue Graves

Illustrated by

Trevor Dunton

W
FRANKLIN WATTS
LONDON • SYDNEY

Tiger was always getting cross. He got cross about **everything**. He got cross if Monkey sat in his favourite seat.

He got cross if
Little Lion got in
his way.

He even got cross if he didn't get jelly
for lunch!

Tiger was **horrid** when he got cross.

He stamped his feet. He shouted and yelled.

He rolled on the floor, too.

Everyone was **scared** of Tiger.
When Tiger had a tantrum,
everyone ran and **hid**.

On Monday, Miss Bird gave out some new colouring pencils. She told everyone to draw pictures of the jungle.

Tiger wanted the red pencil, but Hippo got it first. Tiger got cross. He **snatched** the pencil from Hippo. Hippo was upset.

Miss Bird said that Tiger must give the pencil back. She said he had to wait for his turn for the red pencil.

But he didn't want to wait for his turn. He wanted the pencil **now!** Tiger had a tantrum. He tipped the pencils all over the floor. Miss Bird sent him out of the room to **calm down**.

At playtime, Tiger was still feeling cross. He wanted to play football with Lion. But Lion wanted to play basketball with Little Lion. Tiger snatched the ball and kicked it into the middle of the swamp.

Lion and Little Lion were upset. They told Miss Bird. Miss Bird said Tiger had to go inside and **miss playtime altogether!**

In the afternoon, Miss Bird said she had a nice surprise for everyone. She said they were going to visit Miss Bear at the library to choose new books. Miss Bird said everyone had to walk **nicely** and in twos.

She chose Hippo and Elephant to be the leaders. But Tiger had a tantrum. He wanted to be **the leader**. Miss Bird said he had to walk at the back with her and **be good!**

At the library, Miss Bear showed them lots of books. There were big books and small books. There were fat books and thin books. There were tall books and short books.

Tiger wanted the book about **tractors**. He liked tractors very much. He asked Miss Bear where he could find the book. Miss Bear told him to look on the shelves. She told him to have a **good look**.

Then Tiger saw the tractor book. It was sticking out at the end of the shelf. He tried to reach it but **everyone** was in his way. He got **cross**. He began to push everyone out of his way.

Miss Bird told him **not to push** and to wait nicely for his turn. But Tiger did not want to wait nicely for his turn. He got crosser and **crosser!**

Just then Tiger saw Monkey. He was taking the tractor book off the shelf. Tiger had a **tantrum**. He stamped his feet. He shouted and yelled. He rolled on the floor. He got so cross that he knocked all the books **off the shelf**.

Everyone was scared. They ran and hid.
But Miss Bird and Miss Bear were **not** scared.
They were **not happy** that Tiger was upsetting
everyone else.

Miss Bird took Tiger outside to **talk about it**. She told him to take a deep breath. Tiger took a deep breath. He began to calm down. He felt sad that he had made the library a mess. He felt sad that he had upset everyone.

Miss Bird told him he had to **put** things **right**. She asked him what he should do. Tiger had a think. He said he should say **sorry** to Miss Bear and to everyone. He said he should **tidy up** all the mess in the library. Miss Bird said that they were good ideas.

Tiger said sorry to Miss Bear and to everyone.
He put all the books **neatly** on the shelves.

Then he sat **quietly** on a beanbag and waited
for everyone to finish choosing their books.
But he was sad that he did not have the tractor
book to read.

Then Monkey had a good idea. He asked Tiger if he would like to share the tractor book with him.

Monkey and Tiger looked at the book together. They looked at all the tractors. They talked about them, too. They **took turns** to turn over the pages. They **took turns** to talk about the pictures. Tiger didn't get cross at all.

Miss Bird was pleased. She said Tiger was behaving **nicely**. Tiger said that it was more **fun** to share a book with a friend. He said it was **better** not to get cross, too. Everyone cheered!

A note about sharing this book

The *Behaviour Matters* series has been developed
to provide a starting point for further discussion on
children's behaviour both in relation to themselves
and others. The series is set in the jungle with animal
characters reflecting typical behaviour traits often
seen in young children.

Tiger Has a Tantrum

This story explores the problems that anger and temper tantrums present
not only to the person feeling angry but also the effect these have on others.

The book aims to encourage children to develop coping strategies in
controlling their own anger and to examine ways they could help friends
who might be experiencing similar difficulties to Tiger.

How to use the book

The book is designed for adults to share with either an individual child,
or a group of children, and as a starting point for discussion.

The book also provides visual support and repeated words and phrases to
build reading confidence.

Before reading the story

Choose a time to read when you and the children are relaxed and have
time to share the story.

Spend time looking at the illustrations and talk about what the book might
be about before reading it together.

Encourage children to employ a phonics first approach to tackling
new words by sounding the words out.

After reading, talk about the book with the children:

- What was the story about? Have the children felt angry when a situation has frustrated them, for example having to wait their turn to do something they are particularly excited about? Encourage the children to draw on their own experiences.

- Discuss ways of handling anger and how employing certain strategies may make a person feel calmer, for example, time out; counting to ten; visualisation of their anger; distracting themselves with another activity until the anger passes and so on. Again, ask the children which strategies they have found most useful on a tried and tested basis.

- Take the opportunity to talk about coping with someone who is angry. Point out that, as with Tiger in the story, his anger was not directed at Monkey, but just that he could not have the book himself.

- Talk about the importance of saying 'sorry' to those who have been upset by their actions. Explain how this can make the person feel better.

- Invite two children to role-play the parts of Tiger and Monkey in the story using the strategies for coping with anger that have been discussed. How quickly did the situation resolve using these strategies? Encourage all the children to express their opinions about the effectiveness of them.

Franklin Watts
This edition published in Great Britain in 2016 by The Watts Publishing Group

Series Editor: Jackie Hamley
Series Designer: Cathryn Gilbert

A CIP catalogue record for this book is available
from the British Library.

ISBN 978 1 4451 4718 5 (pbk)
ISBN 978 1 4451 2776 7 (library ebook)

Printed in China

Franklin Watts
An imprint of
Hachette Children's Group
Part of The Watts Publishing Group
Carmelite House
50 Victoria Embankment
London EC4Y 0DZ

An Hachette UK Company
www.hachette.co.uk

www.franklinwatts.co.uk